finders keepers

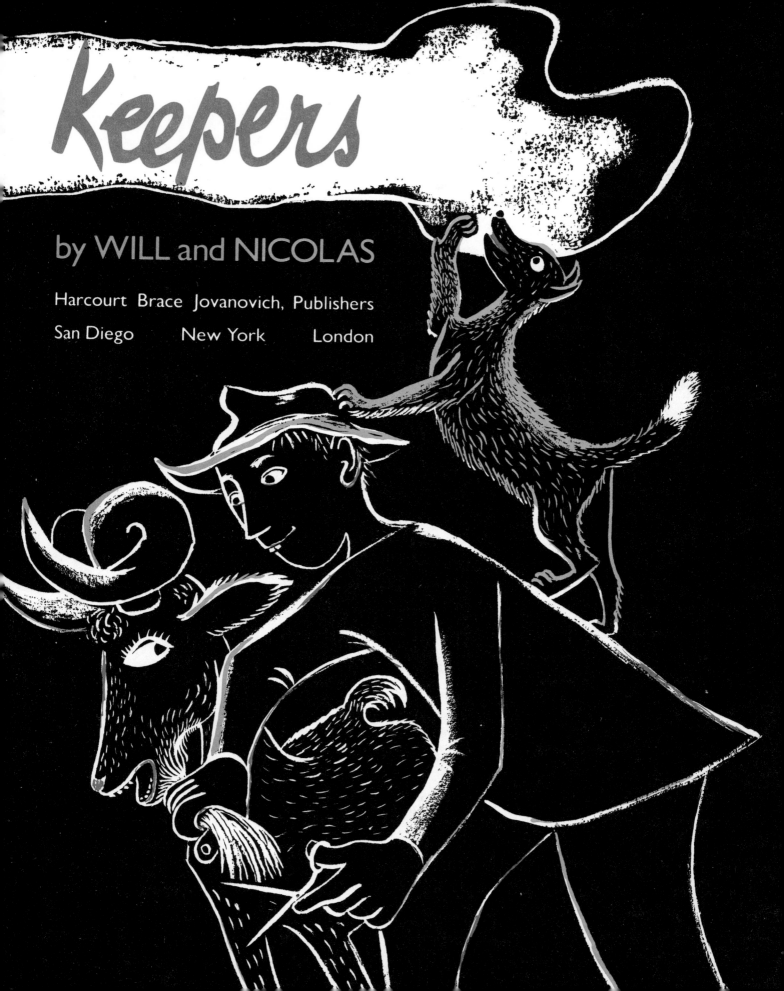

Keepers

by WILL and NICOLAS

Harcourt Brace Jovanovich, Publishers

San Diego   New York   London

HBJ

Requests for permission to make copies of any part
of the work should be mailed to:
Copyrights and Permissions Department,
Harcourt Brace Jovanovich, Publishers,
Orlando, Florida 32887.

Library of Congress Cataloging-in-Publication Data
Will, 1904–1974.
Finders keepers.
Summary: Two dogs each claim a bone they have found
and ask passersby for help in deciding ownership.
[1. Dogs—Fiction]   I. Nicolas, 1911–1973.
II. Title.
PZ7.L6637Fi   1989   [E]   87-8500
ISBN 0-15-227529-0
ISBN 0-15-630950-5 (pbk.)

Y Z
G H I J K (pbk.)

Two dogs were digging in the yard. One had a spot on his head. His name was Nap. The other had a spot on his tail. His name was Winkle. Scratch, scratch. Scratch, scratch. They never stopped digging for a minute. At last they found a bone.

"That bone is mine," said Nap. "I saw it first."

"It's mine," said Winkle. "I touched it first."

Afarmer drove by with a load of hay and his cart bogged in a soft spot on the road.

"Let's ask the farmer," said Nap.

"Suits me," said Winkle. "Whose bone is it, Mr. Haymaker, Nap's or mine? I touched it first."

"But I saw it first," said Nap.

"Just give a hand here at shoving my cart out of the rut and I'll see what I can do," the farmer said.

Nap and Winkle and the farmer and the horse
pushed and pulled and pushed and pulled. And
they hauled the cart out of the rut.

"Now tell us whose bone it is, Nap's or mine," said Winkle.

"Bone?" said the farmer. "Bone? Who cares about a bone? Here's something better than a bone." And he tossed them a forkful of hay.

Nap and Winkle, they looked at the hay and they didn't know what to do.

Just then along came a goat.

"Whose bone is it, Mr. Tuftichin," said Nap, "Winkle's or mine? I saw it first."

"But I touched it first," said Winkle.

"Just let me take care of that nice bit of hay," said the goat, "and I'll see what I can do." He chewed up every wisp of the hay, waggling his beard and looking very thoughtful.

When the goat had shaken all the seeds out of his beard, Nap said, "Now tell us whose bone it is, Winkle's or mine."

"Bone?" said the goat. "Bone? Who cares about a bone? I'll give you some good advice instead. Don't go chasing after a goat unless your teeth are sharper than his horns."

And off he skipped, leaving them no wiser.

Then Nap said, "Let's go down the road a ways and see if we can't find somebody to decide between us."

"Suits me," said Winkle.

They buried the bone and set off down the road. The first person they met was an apprentice barber. He was just learning how to cut hair and couldn't find anybody to practice on.

"Mr. Hairtrimmer," said Nap, "Winkle and I found a bone. Whose should it be, his or mine? I saw it first."

"But I touched it first," said Winkle.

"Just let me trim your hair a bit to try my tools and I'll see what I can do," said the barber.

He went at Winkle's hair with his scissors,
clipping and snipping, while Nap looked on and
smiled.

Then Nap had his hair cut, while Winkle looked
on and smiled.

The barber held his mirror up.

"Suits me," said Winkle, holding himself very straight. Nap laughed.

"Not bad," said Nap, looking very solemn. This time Winkle laughed.

But when they asked about the bone, the barber shrugged his shoulders and said, "Bone? Who cares about a bone? Hair that is neat is better than meat." And he took up his bag of tools and off he went.

Just then a big dog came ambling down the road.

"Nap and I found a bone, Mr. Longshanks," said Winkle. "Whose bone is it, Nap's or mine? I touched it first."

"But I saw it first," said Nap.

"That isn't easy to say," said the big dog, wagging his tail slowly. "What sort of a bone is it?"

"Just an ordinary bone," said Nap.

"Well," said the big dog, wagging his tail a little faster. "You'd better show the bone to me."

Nap and Winkle dug up the bone and the big dog looked at it.

"This is a nice little bone," said the big dog, and his tail went so fast you could hardly see it. "I'll be glad to take care of it for you."

He picked up the bone and
started for the gate. Then
Nap looked at Winkle and
Winkle looked at Nap.

Winkle jumped at the big dog's head, Nap at his tail.

And they bit and they slashed until the big dog
dropped the bone and ran off yelping.

Then Nap looked at Winkle and Winkle looked at Nap. And Nap took one end of the bone and Winkle took the other end of the bone and they both chewed away at it together, without another word.

Winkle and Nap dug and dug, and at last they found a bone. "I saw it first," said Nap. "That bone is mine." "I touched it first. It's mine," said Winkle.

Who would help them to decide? Not Mr. Haymaker, the farmer, for he was interested only in his cart. Not Mr. Tuftichin, the goat, for he was interested only in hay. Not Mr. Hairtrimmer, the apprentice barber, for he only wanted to practice with his scissors. But when Mr. Longshanks, a big mean dog, came along, Nap and Winkle made up their minds in a hurry!

In *Finders Keepers*, the author and artist have collaborated to create a distinguished book, with brilliant and humorous pictures and an original story that will keep children chuckling for a long time to come.

WINNER OF THE CALDECOTT MEDAL

A VOYAGER/HBJ BOOK
HARCOURT BRACE JOVANOVICH, PUBLISHERS
1250 SIXTH AVENUE, SAN DIEGO, CA 92101
111 FIFTH AVENUE, NEW YORK, NY 10003